OPERATION CODE-CRACKER

JOHN TOWNSEND

ILLUSTRATED BY SEAN LONGCROFT

A & C BLACK
AN IMPRINT OF BLOOMSBURY
LONDON NEW DELHI NEW YORK SYDNEY

Contents

Chapter 1
ICURYY4ME

It was there again, somewhere in the darkness of his bedroom. Just beyond the foot of his bed. Moving and breathing. Exactly like the night before.

Heavy with sleep, Max struggled to sit up, squinting into a solid wall of blackness. As his brain swirled in and out of the weird dream, he held his breath so he could hear above the thumping in his chest and the rushing of blood in his head. It was the same dream returning: the one about the old house next door…and the child-catcher lurking somewhere inside.

Max froze. It didn't make sense, but he was certain he wasn't alone. In the stillness of his room he heard the faintest murmur, like a dying sigh. Was it just his dressing gown sliding to the floor from its hook on the door – or something else? Maybe something ready to grab him?

'Who's there? Dad, is it you?'

His croak was swallowed by the stifling darkness.

By now he was shivering. He heard something brush along the foot of the duvet, almost within reach. Apart from the red 01.46 on the clock radio beside his bed, his world was totally black. There wasn't even a grey smudgy outline of the curtains around the window. He stretched his arm to fumble for the switch on the bedside light but his hand struck the lamp, knocking it over in a clatter of dinosaur models. His scrabbling fingers couldn't find the switch.

Groping ham-fistedly through the broken limbs of a triceratops, Max was sure he heard the door whisper over the carpet. His thumb at last hit the switch and light burst across his screwed-up eyelids. From just outside his room, Max heard rustling followed by a creak of a stair. He clambered clumsily over his bed as the front door clicked softly downstairs.

Frozen in terror, he swallowed hard to ease the strangling tightness in his throat.

'Dad? Are you there?'

Max's legs were trembling as he strained to

hear his dad breathing heavily in the next room. Why did his dad always sleep so deeply when it came? But waking him was never a good idea. The last time Max had tried to convince him about the 'thing in the night', Dad had made him feel really stupid.

'For goodness' sake, stop imagining things. You're a bit old to be worried about the bogeyman from under the stairs by now. You'll be eleven soon, for heaven's sake.'

Of course, in the cold light of day, it did seem stupid. Why would anyone creep into his room at night and disappear without a trace? But now he was sure he hadn't imagined it. It was definitely more than a dream. His dream – where he'd been ringing the creepy neighbour's doorbell and the front door flew open, flashing light across his eyes… That was when he'd woken. Suddenly he knew it was a blade of light that had sliced into his dream; torchlight on his eyelids before he'd heard the click of a switch and all went dark.

Max was absolutely certain someone had been creeping around his room with a torch – and an open opportunity to throttle him in his sleep.

With his eyes now accustomed to the light, he sat on his bed and gazed around his room. His dressing gown lay on the floor like a crumpled body, slumped by the slightly open door. He was sure he'd left it shut. The rucksack he brought when he came to stay with his dad was in its usual place on the chair but he knew without doubt he hadn't tied the drawstring at the top. Now it was tied, in a bow. He never did bows.

Even more mysteriously, Max's autograph book was open on the desk. He knew very well he'd closed it just before he'd gone to sleep. The last thing he'd done before getting into bed was to admire a signature from the footballer who'd visited school that day. But now the open page glared at him, for it was the page signed by Gran a few years before:

YY U R
YY U B
I C U R
YY 4 ME
LOL Gran

Even now, Max wasn't sure if the LOL meant 'lots of love' or 'laugh out loud'. The rest of the code still made him smile: 'Too wise you are, too wise you be, I see you are too wise for me.' It had taken him a while to work it out at first but now it seemed very simple.

Max was shivering uncontrollably. He scrambled back into bed, but there was no way he could sleep. What if burglars had broken in? What if Dad's house was haunted? What if the child-catcher had crept in from the big old house next door? The one in his dream.

As he lay with the light still on, staring blankly up at the ceiling, Max was relieved that soon he'd be back home with Mum on the other side of town, when she came back from her holiday. She always said it was the 'not so posh part' but he didn't mind. He'd never been woken in the night in his room there, where he didn't have to worry about a presence by his bed – with a torch.

Grey light eventually began to bleed into his bedroom through the heavy curtains. Birds started calling from the trees, then clattering on the roof as the dawn chorus grew to a crescendo. Max slid out of bed and pulled the curtains back. A blackbird was drinking from a puddle on the flat conservatory roof just below his window. He watched it fly off and perch on the high wooden fence then flutter down onto the lawn next door. He stared in disbelief and sighed. 'That's all I need.'

In the misty dawn light, Max could just make out a shape in the middle of the neighbour's dewy lawn. It was his football. However had it got there?

So now he had two things on his mind:

1. Had he really been woken in the night by an intruder?

2. Did he really have to go to that creepy house next door and ask for his ball back?

Max sighed again, crawled back into bed, pulled the duvet over his head, curled up tightly and tried to get back to sleep. He failed. He dreaded having to uncurl in a couple of hours and go downstairs where his dad would go completely ballistic at discovering they'd been burgled.

But to his immense surprise, on the dot of 7.30, Max heard a cheery call rise from the foot of the stairs: 'Max, up you get – time for Coco Pops!'

Chapter 2
MY TRUANDER ROOM

As soon as Max pressed the neighbour's doorbell, he wished he hadn't. An eerie chime echoed deep inside the rambling house and he desperately wanted to run. It was like his dream all over again. He swallowed hard and braced himself to face the mysterious man who lived behind that door.

Muffled scraping came from the other side of the door, as Max stared up at a peephole set in the varnished wood. A bulging eyeball looked back at him through the glass. A chain rattled, followed by clunks from the lock. Max stepped back, and slipped awkwardly off the doorstep, scraping his shin and grazing the skin. Slowly the door moved, letting daylight spill into the gloomy hallway and brush across the man's face as he emerged from the shadows. A middle-aged face with cold grey eyes and a nose that, seen close up, looked even longer than Max had remembered. It was Gran who'd first described the man as the Child-Catcher in *Chitty Chitty Bang Bang*.

Music seeped out through the open door, together with a strong smell of curry. For a split second Max thought how scary it would be if the music was from *Chitty Chitty Bang Bang*, but it sounded more like Bach. He glanced down, noticing a little wooden cross with R.I.P. on it, just to the left of the doorstep. Its marble base, engraved with the word LOVE, held a single white rose. An odd place for a pet's grave, he thought.

'Sorry to disturb you,' Max began. He'd rehearsed what to say very carefully. 'Would you mind if I get my ball back, please? It seems to have gone over the fence.'

The man moved further out into the light, eyes squinting slightly. 'Seems?' he sniffed.

'Er, yes. My football. It's on your back lawn. Sorry.'

'So there's no 'seems' about it. It's definite. Sounds like you definitely kicked it over.'

'Yes… I mean no. I'm sorry to bother you.'

The man stepped out onto the doorstep. He wore a dark suit and a blue-striped shirt with a navy blue tie.

'When did you do it?' he asked seriously. Too seriously, as far as Max was concerned.

'Er… I'm not really sure,' Max answered, sort of truthfully, bending down to wipe his shin. He screwed up his face as blood smeared the stinging graze.

'Not sure? Not sure? Are you telling me you did it in your sleep?'

This wasn't going very well. Max hadn't rehearsed this bit. 'Maybe this morning,' he lied.

'So you take full responsibility for such foolishness?'

The real answer was undoubtedly NO. Max knew full well he hadn't kicked the ball. He hadn't played with it for days. He just wanted it back, that was all.

'If it's inconvenient, I can leave it for now if you'd rather,' Max heard himself saying.

The man paused as the Bach over his shoulder came to a finale with a flourish.

'Are you going to be in this evening?' he asked, looking very severe. 'With your father?'

Max stared at him blankly. 'Yes. Yes, I think so. Dad should get back at about six.'

'So any time before nine-thirty, then? That's your bedtime, isn't it, Maxwell?'

'Er, usually.' Max felt this conversation was getting weirder by the minute.

'That's quite late enough for a ten-year-old. Early to bed, early to rise, makes a lad healthy, wealthy and wise.' He paused before adding, 'I see you are too wise for me…'

Max stared in disbelief. The man stepped back briskly. 'I'll be round at eight. I might bring the ball.' And he shut the door, leaving Max on the step with a strange feeling in his stomach and a lingering smell of fried onions.

He stood on the doorstep long after the door had closed in his face, trying to make sense of the bizarre conversation. What was the big deal? It was only a tatty old football. So why was there to be an official complaint to Dad at 20.00 precisely? More creepily, how did Child-Catcher know when Max went to bed and how old he was? And another thing: where did 'Maxwell' come from? He'd never been called that in his life, not since the name had been recorded on his birth certificate. It was his mum's maiden name but he'd always been known as just plain 'Max'. In fact, there was no possible reason why Child-Catcher should know his name in the first place. They had never spoken to each other before. Why should they? Max only came to stay with Dad for the odd weekend or when Mum went away with her sister.

All Max knew about the strange neighbour was that he lived alone, was often away on business and seldom seemed to be at home for long. He drove a smart BMW and always wore a suit, even in the garden where he could occasionally be glimpsed trimming the hedge or cutting the lawn when it was getting dark. And now, it seemed, the nutter was intent on coming round to cause an ugly scene, over a football. Max just hoped his dad would handle it calmly without flying into one of his rages. That would be all they needed. Since he'd been stopped yet again by the police for having faulty tyres and then got a speeding ticket, Dad was about to lose his driving licence. He'd become extra edgy and unbearable to live with. Without a car, he said, his career as a medical rep was over.

***

Max's gran told him not to worry. She was always telling people not to worry. She told Max not to worry about the neighbour. 'At least Child-Catcher didn't throw you in a cage or lock you up in his cellar! I'll bring you another ball when I next pop round, dear.'

19

She kissed him on the cheek, called upstairs that she was 'just off' to Max's dad, who'd arrived home more bad-tempered than usual, and went out to her pink Morris Minor convertible parked in the drive. Max waved from the front window as she reversed in fits and starts into the avenue, narrowly missing a Volvo parked opposite. A Volvo with a man inside, who was watching him closely as he waved to Gran. That was odd in itself. Yet, what was more unnerving, Max was sure it was the same car he'd sometimes seen parked outside his school. Just waiting.

Once more Max felt a shiver run down his back. He could only be certain of one thing: something very weird was going on. Or, as he wrote in his secret coded diary:

MY TRUANDER ROOM.

Chapter 3

BCDFHIJKLMOPQRSuVWXYZ X 2

At one minute past eight the doorbell rang. 'That'll be him,' Max said nervously.

'Leave this to me,' his dad sighed, getting up from the sofa, switching off the TV and going out to answer the front door.

Max didn't understand what all the fuss was about. Did a stray football really make him such a bad person? Didn't Child-Catcher have anything better to do than come round and demand an apology? If his dad started swearing and shouting it could all get nasty.

The sitting room door opened and Max's dad returned. 'Come through,' he said. Turning to Max, he muttered, 'He'd like a word with you. Don't worry.' He ushered the neighbour into the room. 'Take a seat.'

Child-Catcher wore the same dark suit and tie as before and carried an attaché case. Perhaps he's a bank manager, Max thought. But why hadn't he brought back the football?

As he sat down, the creepy man looked directly at Max. 'I'll get straight to the point, young man. We need your help.'

Help? Surely it wasn't too difficult to pick up a football and throw it back. And who were 'we'? Was he married?

'Don't look so alarmed,' Child-Catcher went on. 'You could do a very important job for me.'

He opened his case and took out a wad of papers. 'Whether or not you and your father agree to assist, I need to tell you from the outset that you will both have to sign some papers.'

'Whatever for?' Max's dad butted in, already sounding aggressive.

'Just a formality. The Official Secrets Act.'

'It's only a football for heaven's sake!'

'No, Mr Hunter. The football is irrelevant. This is official government business. I'm here in my position as...as, shall we say, a representative of the service, with a request for you. You are at complete liberty to reject my request but I do have to insist that you sign, even before I explain the nature of the operation.'

'Operation? What is this, a grumbling appendix? Or a medical procedure to remove a football from a neighbour's back garden?'

'It would help if you could remain calm and listen to everything I say, Mr Hunter. It could be to your considerable advantage.'

By now Max was more confused than ever. He didn't want all this ridiculous nonsense. All he wanted was his football back. But Child-Catcher looked even scarier under electric light. His balding sweaty forehead glistened, while his slatey eyes remained as cold and calculating as ever. His wispy ginger eyebrows didn't seem to match, with one looking as if it had slipped slightly. He kept one hand in his jacket pocket as if he were concealing a dagger.

'Just explain yourself,' Max's dad said. 'How do you mean, advantage?'

'Shall we just say that I am prepared to influence your disqualification from driving? I can wipe the slate clean for you.'

'How on earth do you know about that?'

'It's my business, Mr Hunter. I work at GCHQ.'

'What's that?' Max spoke for the first time.

'Government communications,' the man said coldly, as if his answer explained everything.

He held his identity card a few centimetres in front of their noses.

'Hush-hush stuff?' Max's dad asked. 'Espionage?'

'I deal with matters of national security and of immense sensitivity, if that's what you mean, Mr Hunter.'

'What, like my driving licence?'

'Or lost footballs?' Max felt even more confused.

'Are you serious about the driving licence?' Max's dad said thoughtfully. 'You can actually get me off the hook?'

'You scratch my back and I'll scratch yours, Mr Hunter. But first I need your signatures.'

With his left hand the man took a pair of gold-rimmed glasses from his inside jacket pocket and delicately placed them on his long nose, then handed papers to Max and Dad, as well as a fountain pen.

'By signing these you are sworn to utter secrecy. These are legal documents and it is vital you both understand that under no circumstances do you discuss or communicate our business with anyone.' He looked directly at Max. 'Do you understand? Not even your mother, grandmother or best friend.'

Max nodded and looked across at his dad who was carefully reading the document.

'All very government-speak,' he said. 'For all you know this room could be bugged.'

'It isn't,' the man said, looking over the top of his glasses. 'We've checked.'

Max was horrified. 'Do you mean someone's been round to have a look for bugs?'

'No need,' Child-Catcher said. 'Remote surveillance is our speciality. That said, we did sweep through this property last weekend while you were both at the football match. All perfectly clean. I check all details about new recruits. I even know what breakfast cereal Maxwell prefers.'

'You can't possibly know that!' Max protested.

The man flicked through some papers in a file. 'According to our records, it seems to be Coco Pops. Correct?'

Dad leaned forward. 'Have you been going through our wheelie bin, by any chance?'

'Of course. Among other things. Supermarket records can be very useful, too. All kinds of records – telephone, emails and websites visited. We know everything about you.'

Max sat up indignantly. 'Have you sent round spies to search my bedroom?'

'Of course not.'

'Like in the middle of the night?'

Child-Catcher's eyes remained focused on his papers. '"Spies" is such a vulgar word. They were civil servants. One was most intrigued by your wide range of reading material. Very promising. A good mix. Non-fiction as well as fantasy fiction. You clearly posses a fertile imagination. Always a good sign in this business. However, your musical tastes leave something to be desired.' There was still no hint of a smile.

'So I was right. There was a bogey man on the prowl in my room, after all.' Max even felt relief that it hadn't been a robber waking him in the early hours. 'Anyway, what's wrong with my musical tastes? Just because I'm not into Bach!'

The man looked up and removed his glasses. His wonky eyebrow rose at one end. 'Bright lad, eh? But not too smart, I hope. There's nothing worse than impudent children who get above themselves. Too wise you be...'

'That's what Gran wrote in my autograph book. YY U B.'

'So I gather. We prefer more subtle and cryptic codes in our business. I'll leave this one for you to solve.' He took a piece of paper from his pocket, and wrote a string of letters on it:

BCDFHIJKLMOPQRSUVWXYZ x 2

While Max tried to make sense of it, Dad carefully read the documents marked 'Top Secret' before signing the last sheet. 'Right, if you've really got the power to lift my driving ban, I'm very grateful, but what's the catch? What do you want from me?'

'There's no catch, I assure you, Mr Hunter. All

I need from you is another signature to give your permission. Nothing more.'

'Permission for what?'

'Permission for Maxwell here to be employed by my department on a certain matter affecting national security.'

Max screwed up his face. 'Whatever does that mean? I'm sure I can't be any use. By the way, my name is Max.'

'Be that as it may,' Child-Catcher said, 'I still need you to sign before I ask you to make your decision.'

Max signed the paper, sat back and asked, 'So what do you want me to do?'

Without saying a word, Child-Catcher collected the signed papers, put the top back on his fountain pen and returned it to his jacket pocket.

'I have chosen you for a number of reasons, Max. Firstly, it has to do with your school and in particular a boy in your class. I want you to find some confidential information. What you might call "top secret". You are sensible and intelligent and I believe you won't let us down. We've been watching you closely for the last few weeks. I was also impressed by the way you asked for your ball back – seeing as you hadn't kicked it over. It was

I who placed it on my lawn. And you didn't make a fuss about grazing your leg on my step – the first thing I saw when I opened my door to you earlier. All good signs. I can't stand children who make a fuss.'

'You mean that football was a test? If I'd known, I'd have been less polite!'

Child-Catcher ignored Max's remark. 'How well do you know a boy called Jay in your class?'

'I thought you knew everything about me.' Max grinned. 'He's okay. He's cool.'

'Have you ever been to his house?'

'Not inside, no. I've called round for him a couple of times.'

'Splendid. Under no circumstances must you tell Jay of our suspicions. He has an uncle, his mother's brother, who has just entered the country…'

'Yes, I know,' Max said. 'His Uncle Kurt has been staying in their spare room for a week. He's got a daughter, Miya, about my age.'

'We need to know a great deal more about him. We are working with the CIA and Interpol who believe he is a major player in a terrorist organisation. We need to know what he is planning so that we can round up all his contacts, preferably catching them red-handed with all evidence against them intact. We therefore need someone like you to become a trusted member of the family circle.'

'Hold on a minute,' Max's dad stood up. 'You want my son to infiltrate a gang of terrorists? How dangerous is this?'

Child-Catcher thought for a few seconds. 'I would be lying if I said there was no risk whatsoever. But Max will not be working alone. He will have the complete back-up of British Intelligence. And of course, with a successful conclusion to the operation, I needn't tell you of the financial reward on offer. Enough, shall we say, to pay off your mortgage and guarantee a healthy future for Max.'

'I'm more concerned about the welfare and safety of my son. What if he gets hurt?'

Child-Catcher paused while he wiped his forehead with a crisp white handkerchief. 'Then I'm afraid we will deny all knowledge of his – and our – involvement. But I assure you I foresee no likely problems. All Max has to do is listen carefully, take a careful note of details and report back. Mission accomplished.'

'You're asking a lot, you know.' Max's dad sat down again, looking flustered.

'I realise this will have little effect on your decision but it would assist the national interest, indeed the safety, of the entire country. Possibly world peace. Such service is rewarded in all kinds of ways. Max's prospects for the future, in whatever career he chooses to follow, would be significantly enhanced…'

It was Max's turn to stand up. He stretched out his arm ready for a handshake. 'I'll do it,' he said proudly. 'I'm your man!'

Dad touched his arm. 'Steady, Max. Let's just think about this.'

'It's okay, Dad. I want to. If I can get you driving again and make you happy, that's good enough for me. And if I can stop Jay getting hurt by all this stuff, I want to help. Anyway, I think I could do a good job – it sounds exciting.'

'I need to make clear a few more points,' Child-Catcher said. 'Firstly, there must be no communication between us as neighbours. You must not contact me directly next door. I shall make contact with you if I need to. I will return here shortly for an official briefing. Secondly, whilst my department will be on call at any time, there are strict procedures. You have to abide by firm rules and use the correct channels. From now on you must only refer to me as Delta.'

Dad laughed. 'I've always thought of you as

just plain "Mr Nettles from next door". It's all a bit James Bond for my liking.'

Max jumped to his feet, whistling the Bond theme tune and posing with his hands shaped like a gun. Delta clearly didn't approve. 'Let's just keep this in perspective, Max. This isn't glamorous or clever. It will need skill on your part. Cunning and courage. After all, this case is a serious nut we've got to crack.'

'So are you telling me I'm no more than a nut case?'

There was almost a glimmer of a smile on Delta's face. He wiped his left palm on his handkerchief, folded it precisely and returned it to his breast pocket.

'So far the case has only been given a letter. Operation C. We'll have to think of a suitable name beginning with C at some point. Something snappy.'

'Can I choose?' Max asked.

'I don't see why not. Any suggestions?'

'How about "Operation Child-Catcher"?'

Dad stifled a laugh.

'Any particular reason?' Delta asked, snootily.

Max looked at Dad with a cheeky snigger. 'Not particularly. It just sounds cool.'

'I beg to differ,' Delta sneered, writing the title

on his file. He was left-handed and the writing was tiny and precise. 'I don't approve of such a name. Think again.' He crossed out 'Child-Catcher' and printed something above it. 'Do you have any other questions to ask me, Max?'

'Now you come to mention it, there is just one thing.'

'What is it?'

Max took a deep breath. 'Any chance of having my football back, please?'

Delta looked up, expressionless, before he finally smiled.

'I'll pop round tomorrow to give final instructions and I'll return it. I'll see then if you've worked out that puzzle.' He pointed to the weird message on the paper. 'In fact, I might bring you another brain-teaser. Then we'll see if you're really as bright as they say.'

'I wrote this in code,' Max said. He showed him:

MY TRUANDER ROOM.

'Rather simple,' Delta sneered again. 'AN in TRUDER...in MY ROOM. "AN INTRUDER IN MY ROOM". Easy. You'll have to do better than that. Codes and cryptic anagrams are my

33

business. My I SPY AT LICE. That's an anagram of SPECIALITY.'

He scribbled on a blank sheet of paper and studied it for a few seconds before smiling and writing vigorously. 'An anagram of OPERATION CHILD-CATCHER,' he said smugly, 'is TOP CHILDREN ARE CHAOTIC. That will never do. Besides, given our interest in word puzzles, we ought to call this "Operation Code-Cracker" instead. It has a better ring to it and I shall find it less offensive.' He stared at Max knowingly. There was an embarrassed silence.

Delta stood to offer his hand and as they all secretively shook hands, they repeated the name of their mission with great seriousness and in hushed whispers.

'Operation Code-Cracker.'

Max said no more. He wasn't so sure now. He'd much preferred his first title and he already knew this mission was unlikely to go all his own way. Things seemed beyond his control from the very start.

Chapter 4
xmascara

At exactly one minute past eight the following evening, Delta returned. Once again dressed in a dark suit and silk tie and clutching his attaché case, he entered the sitting room and sat opposite Max, shuffling his feet to ensure his black shiny shoes were aligned and the toes exactly level with each other.

'No second thoughts, I trust?' he asked matter-of-factly, while rummaging through his papers.

'We've discussed this fully,' Dad butted in. 'Max seems more than happy to be your ears and eyes. I've got no reason to doubt his decision so yes, we're still up for this.'

'I've even had a few words with Jay.' Max smiled, as Delta's eyebrow rose nervously. 'Don't worry, I've not given anything away. He's coming here for a sleepover next Saturday night. Dad said he could come with us to football and back here for a take-away and DVD. Then I might get invited back to his house.'

Delta looked at Dad for confirmation. Dad smiled as if to say 'I told you so.' He'd been in a far better mood since his threat of a driving ban had been magically lifted. 'A small price to pay for a clean driving licence! Can I get you a drink, Mr... er... Delta?'

'Not for me. Regarding your licence, the paperwork is already being processed. Your penalties have been erased from the records as I promised. I'm glad to hear Max is already forming bonds with Jay but I have to warn you that his uncle is a different kettle of fish. You will soon find what a slippery character he is.'

'All very fishy!' Max joked.

'What if your intelligence about this man is wrong?' Dad asked.

'It isn't,' Delta snapped. 'We're professional. The Government never deals in shoddy intelligence. So just make sure this man doesn't fool you with any false charm. He's planning something sinister and we need to find out exactly what as soon as possible. I shall also give you a list of things I want you to look for around the house and garden. Any likely bomb-making equipment must be reported to us immediately.'

'Bombs?' Max looked shocked. 'That sounds a bit scary.'

'This isn't a jolly little adventure, Max. This is ugly terrorism in the raw and it's a cruel business. Innocent people get hurt. He's bound to have weapons of some sort. Your job is to find details, clues and evidence.'

'Why don't you just send round your people to check things out?' Dad asked.

'With respect, Mr Hunter, you had no idea that we'd been round this house with a fine-tooth comb simply because you're not a professional terrorist. He'll be prepared. He'll have counter-surveillance equipment and if he gets wind that we're on to him, he'll go to ground and we'll risk losing him. No, by far the best intelligence will be gathered by someone on site while he's actually in the house and off his guard. Someone who isn't seen as a threat. That's why Max must know just what to do and what he can safely use. That's essential and that's why I'm here now.' He looked down at his shoes again, before taking a small package from his case and placing it carefully on the coffee table.

'These are the tools of your trade, Max. I will now explain how and when to use them. Any chance of that drink, Mr Hunter? Earl Grey tea, if you have it.'

'Er…might have… I think we've got some bags somewhere.'

'No milk or sugar. Just a slice of lemon. In a cup, no mug. Bone china preferred.'

Dad pulled a face and left the room, leaving Max with a smile and a lot of questions.

'How will I pass on any information to you?' he asked enthusiastically.

'Not me,' Delta snapped. 'You communicate with Department 42. After today, all communication between you and me terminates once and for all. The name of your contact at Department 42 is Tango. He's head of the team for Operation Code-Cracker.'

Delta leaned forward slowly. Thinking he was about to examine the state of his shoes again, Max sat back to wait. Instead, Delta spoke in a whisper so Max had to strain to hear.

'I've told you before about saying nothing to anyone else about what you hear and see. That also means keeping everything secret from your father as well. As they used to say in the Second

World War, "Even the walls have ears. Careless talk costs lives." If your cover is ever blown by careless talk, you will be in great danger. I needn't tell you that the Silver Scorpion stops at nothing to dispose of enemies, or anyone who upsets them.'

'Silver Scorpion?'

'Jay's Uncle Kurt is a dangerous member of this poisonous organisation that aims to strike at the heart of world governments. Just like a real scorpion's venom, their attacks destroy the very nervous system of civilised society.'

'One Earl Grey with lemon,' Dad announced triumphantly as he entered with a tray of cups and slices of Gran's coffee and walnut sponge. 'Anyone for cake?'

Delta eyed the cake as if it were laced with Silver Scorpion venom. 'I think not.' He pushed the package on the table to Max, who took out the contents.

'It looks like a sort of screwdriver,' Max said, unimpressed.

'It's an electric pick-gun that runs on batteries. It can pick most locks in a matter of seconds, should you need to investigate behind normal household locked doors. It's a clever piece of kit and works on standard padlocks as well.'

'Cool!' Max looked at the next object. 'My own phone. Brilliant!'

'It will only work when you key in your code and fingerprint recognition as it's essential no one else uses it or gets access to your files. You can text, email or phone Tango as well as send image information. Its camera also records flash-free infra-red images for use in total blackout, plus video and sound; and it has internet access. We can send you images of suspects, instructions or coded messages if necessary. A most helpful piece of equipment. Just be warned, Silver Scorpion is a highly organised network with sophisticated technology as well as ruthless operators. At all times be on your guard. I'll give you a couple of these just in case.' He placed two small devices on the table, each with a neckband attached. 'These look like any computer memory sticks that can be worn round the neck. In fact, each is a small distress flare – a mini firework, if you like. It only burns for a matter of seconds but it emits great heat and light so never ignite within ten metres of your face. By pulling out this pin, you have ten seconds before it explodes with a bright flash, sufficient to signal or alert rescue services in the dark.'

Max picked one up to examine. 'Wow – wicked!'

Delta frowned disapprovingly. 'These should only be used in extreme emergencies, never for cheap tricks.'

An awkward silence followed, with Max being lost for words. He glanced down at a scrap of paper on the coffee table. Delta leaned forward and asked, 'I don't suppose you got anywhere solving my puzzle? But there again, I don't suppose a boy your age would have the maturity or skill – '

'Actually,' Max grinned, 'I reckon it's quite easy. I'm really into dingbats.'

Delta's frown deepened.

'Dingbats are special word puzzles,' Dad said. 'My mother gave Max a dingbat game for Christmas. He beats me every time!'

Max fetched the paper with Delta's puzzle written on it:

BCDFHIJKLMOPQRSUVWXYZ x 2

'The missing letters from the alphabet spell A GENT. At first I thought that meant something about a man gone missing. Then I realised it's more likely to do with spies so it probably means MISSING AGENT. Could the "x 2" mean DOUBLE? Maybe MISSING DOUBLE AGENT.

To be honest, I'm not really sure what a double agent is!'

'Spot on,' Delta nodded thoughtfully. 'Most encouraging. A double agent is no more than a traitor – someone who pretends to work for one side while really serving the other. We don't tolerate that sort.'

Max sat back smugly. 'Yay, I cracked it! Now I've got one for you. What saying is this?' He held up some paper with a single word on it:

xmasCara

'I would imagine it has nothing to do with Christmas,' Delta said. 'Nor anyone called Cara. Apart from being an anagram of "A Max Scar", I think it is safe to say...'

Suddenly he looked up. His icy eyes darted in all directions and his wispy eyebrow quivered.

'Is something the matter?' Dad asked. 'Something wrong with the tea?'

'I think my dingbat has stumped him!' Max laughed.

'Sssh. Is there anyone else in the house? A new pet, perhaps?'

'Just Dad and me.'

But Delta's next words were like something from

a spy film. At first Max thought he was trying to be funny – but Delta didn't do humour.

'We're not alone. Someone's there.'

There was a moment's silence while everyone listened intently. They all jumped at a rattle from the kitchen.

'Maybe I didn't put the cake tin back properly. It's probably just slipped a bit on the shelf,' Dad whispered unconvincingly.

But then came a scraping from the kitchen.

Clutching the tray in front of him like a shield and gripping the cake knife, Dad opened the door from the sitting room and approached the kitchen. Max followed close behind, armed only with his new phone with its hot-line to Tango at GCHQ. Not that it would do much good right now.

Dad slowly placed his hand on the door handle, took a deep breath and barged into the kitchen. There was a scream and the smash of a plate.

'Whatever do you think you're doing?' It was a woman's voice. Gran.

'Blimey, Mum! I thought we had burglars. What are you doing here?'

Still startled and with her hand clutching her chest, Gran spluttered and waved her other hand across her face like a fan.

'Goodness me, dear. You scared the living daylights out of me rushing in like that. And you, Max – it looks as if you've seen a ghost. I told you I'd pop back with a chocolate cake when I'd done some baking. Shame about that plate. Sorry, love.'

'It's okay, Gran, it's just that we thought there was an intruder on the loose.'

'Come through for a cuppa, Mum, and a piece of cake. Leave that broken plate, it doesn't matter. We've got a visitor for you to meet.'

Max shook his head frantically. 'Dad, no. Hush hush.'

'A visitor?' Gran laughed. 'Not a new lady friend, darling? This I must see...'

She entered the room and looked round. 'Oh. I knew it was too good to be true.'

Max and his dad stared at the empty chair. Delta was nowhere to be seen. The chair and cushion where he'd been were not creased in the slightest, his cup and saucer had gone completely and there was nothing to suggest he had ever been in the room. He had disappeared without trace.

'A professional to the last,' Dad muttered, going to the front door to peer outside.

'Stop all this nonsense.' Gran sighed. 'I don't know what's got into you both. Now you'll be delighted to know I've brought you a new ball, Max. It's in my bag in the kitchen, dear. Oh look, there's a little package on the sofa. What's in there, I wonder?'

Max dived onto the sofa and grabbed it before Gran could pick it up. 'Just a couple of things to help with a little job I have to do,' he said. 'Ah, he's done my dingbat!'

He picked up the paper with Delta's answer scribbled on it. It said under XMASCARA: 'Could be XLIPSTICK or XBLUSHER. Answer still the same: Kiss and make-up'.

45

'He worked it out.' Max grinned.

Gran frowned. 'You seem to be talking in riddles today, Max. Sometimes I think you've got an over-active imagination. But I wouldn't have you any other way, love.' She ruffled his hair. 'Maybe you get it from me. Perhaps I've got a mad imagination, too. I think that's what the police thought when I phoned them today.'

'You did what? Why?' Dad looked horrified.

'Well, you hear so many stories these days that I felt I had to report it. I was convinced I was being followed in Archers, the garden centre on the ring road. It was a man with a face shaped like a potato who wore grubby tennis shoes – the same man who I've seen staring at me from a white Volvo outside my house for the last couple of weeks. A shifty-looking type. And I'll tell you another thing. This morning I caught him snooping through my wheelie bin. I waved my rolling pin and he ran off but ever since, I've had that uneasy feeling that I'm being watched. And the awful part is, it's just the same in this house. Between you and me, it feels as though something scary is going on. Something very scary indeed – just you mark my words.'

Chapter 5

Must get here
Must get here & WONADLEIRCLEAND
Must get here

On the day after their sleepover, Jay asked Max back to his house to try out some new games on his PlayStation. 'I don't know if my uncle or cousin will be in,' Jay said.

'Cousin?' Max asked.

'Uncle Jay's daughter, Miya. Don't mention her mum. I never knew Auntie Yasmin but she died in some sort of accident a few weeks ago. I think that's why they came to this country but we don't really talk about it.'

Jay lived in a cul-de-sac on an estate near school. The house was hidden behind a high conifer hedge, which made the rooms inside gloomy even on sunny days. The hedge was so thick that Jay could easily climb right inside and hide from his mum when she was in one of her moods. A letter from the council telling her the hedge needed cutting down had just put her in a worse mood than ever.

'Look at that hedge. I ask you, what's wrong with it? I refuse to cut it down,' were the first and only words she said to Max as he came in. But it made him wonder. Maybe that hedge was the reason he'd been called in – he was the only way to see through it.

He glanced around the dark sitting room, wondering if he'd catch sight of the evil terrorist skulking in the gloom. Instead, he saw a cheery-looking girl watching a cartoon on TV. The smell of toast wafted from the kitchen.

'Hi!' she called. 'You must be Max. I'm Miya. Help yourself to toast.'

Max couldn't help staring at her. It wasn't so much her smiling face that surprised him, though it was certainly not what he expected from a terrorist's daughter. What really fascinated him was her voice.

She read his mind. 'American,' she said with a chuckle. 'Everywhere from the mid-west, New York to Dallas. Smart memory stick!'

'Yeah.' Max felt embarrassed. His first day as a spy, and within seconds the distress flare round his neck was clear for all to see. He poked it back inside his shirt. 'It's new,' he mumbled. 'I'm always forgetting my memory stick. Ironic, isn't it?'

She erupted into giggles. 'You're cute! See you later.' She returned to the world of a cartoon shoot-out, with a blast of ricocheting bullets filling the entire house. Max just hoped the noise wouldn't bring her terrorist father running in waving a submachine gun and hurling grenades in all directions.

He turned and found himself face to face with the man himself – the very one he'd been sent to investigate. At first, in the dark hallway, all Max could see was the man's shadowy outline.

'Hi there, young man,' he said brightly. He was holding a piece of buttered toast.

'Hi,' Max replied nervously. 'I'm Max.'

'Security, by any chance?' The man bit into the toast, with a spray of crumbs and butter.

'Pardon?' Whatever did the man mean? Did he already know something?

'Max security,' he chuckled. 'Just like this place, with my sister as chief jail warder! With a bit of luck you've come to help me dig an escape tunnel.'

'Don't worry about Uncle Kurt,' Jay piped up. 'He's nutty as pecan pie, with a dollop of peanut butter on top.'

Uncle Kurt ruffled Jay's hair with his buttery hand before disappearing into the sitting room, with its hail of cartoon bullets and canned laughter.

'Actually, Uncle Kurt's cool,' Jay whispered. 'Mum's been a lot better since he arrived. Come on, let's go up to my room for a battle of wits.'

Max would rather have joined the others in the sitting room. He liked cartoons and toast. And he liked Uncle Kurt and Miya, despite their secret world and the Silver Scorpion. He remembered Delta's warning not to be fooled by the man's charm. Even so, Max couldn't help thinking he seemed like a very friendly sort of terrorist.

Just as Jay switched on his PlayStation and began explaining the wonders of his latest game, a voice called up the stairs. It was Miya.

'Hey, you guys, come on down. We've got plans.'

Max was down in the sitting room like a shot, to join all the other shots still blasting from the TV.

'Just turn that down a tad, Miya,' her dad said, chewing the last of his toast. 'Now, you guys, how do you fancy going to see a movie? I'll treat us all to whatever you want to see and as much popcorn as you can manage. What do you reckon? What kind of thing do you like, Max?'

Jay laughed, 'Anything to do with dingbats. Dingbats, the Movie!'

'Not another word freak,' Kurt teased. 'Miya does ten crosswords before breakfast!'

She was already on her feet and scrawling a coded message on a notepad.

'There you go, wise guy. Try this.'

Max read the words in front of him:

Must get here
Must get here   WONADLEIRCLF AND
Must get here

'Blimey, I haven't got a clue.' He scratched his head.

'Try Jay's room,' she called as she ran up the stairs.

'Hey, what are you doing in my room?' Jay chased her up the stairs, making the sound of a siren.

Max followed on his heels and threw himself, panting, on the bed. 'Can I look at your bookshelf?'

'Sure.'

Max scanned the titles and pulled out two books with a triumphant laugh. 'Got 'em!' He threw one onto the bed. 'If I'm not mistaken, Miya, that book called *The Three Musketeers* is what you mean by MUST GET HERE, MUST GET HERE, MUST GET HERE. As in three "must get here's". And the other clue has the word ALICE hidden in the word WONDERLAND. So you must be referring to the classic ALICE IN WONDERLAND, which of course should really be *Alice's Adventures in Wonderland*.' He grinned smugly.

'Yeah, Mr Clever Guy – but who said I never cheat?' Miya called from the door. 'But well done, Max, you're quick. I guess we're on the same wavelength.'

Jay looked on, totally baffled. 'I'd never have worked that out in a month of Sundays. You two are wordy nerds! You think alike. Fair play, very clever – but completely useless!'

***

52

Within an hour they were sitting in the cinema, with Max between Miya and her dad. Jay sat on the end, his mum having stayed at home to sleep off another of her headaches. As the screen crackled to life with speckled pin-pricks of light that suddenly burst to flash across their faces, Max sank back in his seat, feeling a real glow inside. This was great, and the people with him were great, too. He knew he had an important job to do for the good of the whole country, but Uncle Kurt couldn't really be that dangerous, could he? He seemed so friendly and great fun to be with. Maybe Delta had got things wrong.

A funny advert swirled in front of them. A cartoon frog hopped across the screen with sparks of coloured light peppering the darkness, and an exploding monster lit up the whole cinema with blinding white light and loud farting splats. Everyone laughed. Max chuckled as he looked along the row of seats at all the smiling faces gazing up at the screen. This all felt safe and cosy - a world away from the world of dangerous terrorists... until he caught a glimpse of someone at the far end of the row. It was a man sitting on his own and, for a brief moment, he had been staring intently at Max. And the strangest thing of all, the man was wearing dark glasses – in the middle of a darkened cinema.

Max was sure he'd seen that face before, and that head shaped like a potato. He looked back up at the screen and remembered where he'd seen that outline of a double chin. It had been behind the window of a white Volvo estate.

Max suddenly felt annoyed that Department 42 didn't trust him after all. If the man with the double chin was watching Uncle Kurt, then why had Delta asked Max to do the job? It was ridiculous that the man on the end of the row was meant to be keeping an eye on things, but he couldn't even keep out of sight himself. What sort of a spy was that? Max wanted to tell Tango this man's presence could make his own job more difficult. The trouble was, he couldn't refer to him as 'the man with the double chin' or 'Potato-head'. No, he would have to be more professional and show the evidence. He would photograph him with his special phone that was able to take pictures in the dark.

Max discreetly pulled out his phone, tapped in the code and pressed his finger onto the pad. He selected 'camera' and 'infra-red' before whispering that he was just popping to the loo. He shuffled along the row, pointing the lens at the potato-shaped head just in front of him. As the camera clicked, the man looked up, grunted and scuttled off up the aisle like a startled rat, disappearing into the darkness behind the ice-cream queue. His whole body was like a huge potato, Max thought. Baked, tough-skinned and greasy.

When Max returned to his seat, Uncle Kurt was already handing round the Cornettos. They began peeling off the wrappers as the lights dimmed again and the title of the film appeared in front of them with a loud fanfare. Kurt cheered and acted as the biggest child of them all – until, as the screen brightened and lit up everyone's faces, he glanced across to the end of the row and froze. Max looked to where he was staring and was horrified to see Potato-head was in his seat again, and coldly glancing back at them. Kurt clearly knew him.

'Stop, all of you,' Kurt hissed. 'Don't eat your ice creams.' He held up his wrapper and examined it carefully. 'Give them to me. I'll get some more. These have been tampered with. Whatever you do, don't eat any.'

Miya was just about to take a large bite. 'Hey, Dad – are you crazy?'

'Just listen to me carefully, all of you,' he whispered. 'I'll explain later. Right now I'm going to tell you something important. Keep looking at the movie and listen to me. I'm really sorry, but we've got to get out of here. Don't ask questions now – just act normally. When I count to three we're going to stand quickly and get out as fast as we can. We'll run straight up the gangway, through the foyer, out into the street. Just keep following me. I'll tell you why once we're out of here. Right now, just treat the whole thing as a bit of a fun race. Trust me kids. One…two…three.'

Without stopping to question why, caught up in Uncle Kurt's crazy game, the three children sprang to their feet with a clatter of seats springing back. They shuffled into the middle aisle then darted towards the exit. Potato-head looked confused before he too stood and headed for the green exit sign nearest to him. Faces turned to stare briefly but quickly returned to the more colourful action on the screen.

Max burst out into the foyer, squinting like a mole tunnelling up into daylight. They rushed past the queue waiting for another film and tumbled out onto the pavement where they threw their ice creams in a bin. Kurt sped down the street like the Pied Piper, followed by a line of bewildered children. Max glanced back to see Potato-head emerge from the cinema, looking breathless and exasperated that he couldn't catch them. Kurt led them round a corner and headed down the next street before looking back over his shoulder.

'OK, you guys, we can stop running now. Well done – you'll make the Olympics yet. Sorry about missing the movie. I'll take you back some time, don't worry.'

He paused to catch his breath. 'Right now, I'll treat you to some fries and a milk shake. I know a little place round here so follow me...' He led them down steps into a narrow passageway, along a side alley and into a small courtyard. There was a gloomy little café with no customers inside, just a fog of fumes.

'Don't worry about my dad,' Miya said calmly. 'We're always doing crazy things. Like at the airport we had to hide for an hour in a rest room. You get used to it after a while.'

Jay was still panting furiously. 'There's never a dull moment with Uncle Kurt around!'

Max was full of questions but he knew he'd have to wait for answers. Even so, he felt it was time to contact Tango and warn them Uncle Kurt had recognised Potato-head. As they entered the café, he muttered, 'I just need to wash my hands,' and escaped to the toilet. As soon as he was on his own, Max sent a message as well as the photo of Potato-head.

Kurt has seen this agent and recognises him. Please advise.

Within seconds, as he was returning the phone to his pocket, it bleeped and a message appeared:

Tango to Max. Message received. WARNING. Image of suspect is not – REPEAT NOT – an agent of this department. URGENT – be on your guard. Details of image supplied:
Name: Agent NERO of Silver Scorpion.
Category: Highly dangerous.

Max read the message several times. This didn't make sense. What was going on? If Potato-head was Nero of the Silver Scorpion, why had he been following Max and Gran from that white Volvo for the last week? And why ever should he cause Uncle Kurt to react like that? Max put the phone back in his pocket and looked in the mirror. 'Your mission is to find out,' he said to himself, and returned to the café with its sizzling burgers and belching fumes.

As they sat eating chips and drinking Coke, Uncle Kurt spoke directly to Max.

'I guess you must think your friend has a real weird uncle, eh? Who in their right mind takes a bunch of kids to the movies only to make them throw their ice creams in the trash can and run from the theatre just as the movie's about to start? The thing is, I'm kinda embarrassed and I'd prefer it if you said nothing about this. You see, I owe a guy some money and he sent one of his guys to get it just now. It could've gotten scary back there so I reckoned it was best to get right outta there. That ice cream thing was just to get you kids hyped-up so you'd run like crazy! Thanks, you guys, for being so cool about it.'

'I told you Uncle Kurt's a nutter, didn't I?' Jay smiled.

'We've both been a bit on edge since Mom...' Miya looked unusually serious but her father butted in and stopped her.

'Yeah, well, I don't suppose Max here wants to hear all our family stuff. It's great having you with us, Max. It'll be good to get to know you a bit more.' He beamed a smile as he sat back and drummed his fingers on the table.

'Yeah,' Max said genuinely. 'And I'd like to

know more about you, too. But maybe not too much or I might get some shocks with all your secrets!' He waited for a reaction.

Kurt didn't seem phased in the least. 'You bet.' He laughed and continued drumming his fingers. 'My cupboards are full of scary skeletons.'

'More like dust, webs and spiders,' Miya added.

Max couldn't resist taking a big risk. He spoke before he really had time to think.

'Spiders? I like arachnids. Especially scorpions.' He sipped his drink, without looking at anyone directly. In the short silence that followed, he sensed just the slightest reaction in Kurt's drumming fingers. Jay and Miya continued eating, oblivious.

'So you're into arachnids are you, Max?' Kurt said. 'In the States we had a few interesting ones. We were having a picnic once in Texas when a black widow crawled over the back of my hand. Remember that, Miya?'

'Yeah. Mom screamed. You can get brown widows, too. Not many people know that.'

Max decided to push things even further. If he was to find out more from Kurt, it was time to signal that he knew something about him. It was a risk but he was going to set the bait.

'Arachnids come in all colours but I think the

brighter ones tend to be more dangerous.' He paused before the punch line. 'Scorpions as well. Especially silver.'

This time he looked directly at Kurt and immediately noticed a flash in his eyes. There was a startled stare and a look which clearly said, 'We'll talk later.'

Jay and Miya were too concerned with their chips to notice.

***

'I suggest we head right back and watch a movie at home, how's that?' Kurt said when everyone had finished eating.

'So long as you don't run off again, Dad.' Miya put her arm through his as they left the café and headed back to the street. Max and Jay followed behind as a few spots of rain freckled the pavement and a cool wind dribbled a plastic bottle along the kerb. Max jumped over it as they crossed the street to look in the window of a bike shop. Half-way across the street they heard the roar of an engine and squeal of tyres. A car was racing straight at them. Kurt yelled at the top of his voice and passers-by looked up in horror.

'Run! Get to the sidewalk!'

Max and Jay grabbed each other and hurled themselves onto the path. But the vehicle was on them, mounting the pavement with a clatter of metal and a spray of sparks. Max dived into the shop doorway as Jay was snatched from his grip and smashed across the bonnet of the car. He thumped into the windscreen, which shattered in an instant, the glass crackling into a frosted mosaic.

Jay slid across the car and thudded onto the tarmac. The car swerved off the path and roared away up the street, leaving a shower of glass and smoke. Black tyre-marks smouldered across the pavement but the scream of the fast-disappearing wheels was drowned by Miya's shrieks, as her father held her against the shop window. Max ran to Jay, who lay twisted and motionless in the road, with blood trickling from his head and nose. His face was studded with tiny slivers of glass.

A man called from across the street, 'Did someone get his number?'

Max knew it wasn't necessary. He knew who the driver was, all right. It was Potato-head, Nero of the Silver Scorpion...the hired killer behind the wheel of the dreaded white Volvo estate.

Chapter 6
HOROBOD BAL

'I think it's time we had that talk,' Kurt said to Max in the hospital waiting room.

Looking down at a squashed fly on the lino, Max braced himself for what was to come next. He slowly looked up at Kurt, who sighed and asked with genuine concern, 'How are you? Are you coping okay with all this stuff? I feel so responsible. This mess is all my fault. Jay's mom still hasn't spoken to me since he's been in intensive care. That's almost a week. She's hardly left his bedside, which is understandable. I don't know where I'd be without Miya keeping me together. She's coping so well – especially after all she's gone through lately.'

It was clear that Kurt was desperate to talk. But Max knew there was unfinished business between them, since that knowing look back in the café.

'I know it's horrible seeing Jay all wired up with tubes and things,' Max said, trying to sound as positive as he could, 'but since he came out of the coma, at least they're now saying he's "stable" rather than "critical" so that's a step in the right direction.'

'Yeah, a crumb of comfort, I guess,' Kurt sighed again. 'Despite a concussion, internal injuries and broken bones, he's stable! Poor kid. I just want him home again.'

A woman in a pink overall slopped a mop over the floor and steadily squelched nearer, her wet arcs across the lino soon licking their feet and wiping away the splattered fly. The smell of disinfectant grew ever stronger, setting a man who sat opposite sneezing. He began flicking through a magazine and snuffling into a tissue but he was obviously listening to their conversation and giving them puzzled glances.

'Look, we can't talk here,' Kurt said. 'Shall we go somewhere?'

Miya appeared beside them, as if by magic, looking more cheerful than she'd been for a while. She'd been badly shaken by Jay's horrific hit and run.

'I've been having a little chat with Jay,' she said. 'They're going to do some more tests. There's also talk of putting a pin and stuff in his leg. It's pretty smashed up – they showed us the x-ray. Can I stay here with his mom for a while? There's no real point you guys staying all day. Why not come back in a couple of hours? Get some air – it looks like a nice day out there.'

'We might do that if you're okay staying here,' Kurt said. 'Max and I were thinking about what to do. We'll go for a stroll and a chat. Maybe walk into town. What d'you reckon?'

'That's fine by me,' Max nodded. 'Miya, just tell Jay we'll be back to keep an eye on him. Warn him I might tell him one of my jokes. Or a few dingbats.'

***

As Max walked out into the dazzling sunlight, he was in a swirl of strange feelings. Not many days ago he'd hardly known Jay and had never even heard of Miya or her dad. Now he suddenly felt close to them, sharing all their worries and fears. Thanks to a white Volvo everything had changed. A Volvo, and a maniac who was still out there. Max feared Nero would strike again.

A warm breeze stirred the trees, which were

vibrant with colour – unlike the drab waiting room with its dull plastic spider plant, dead fly and grey sloppy mop.

'Let's sit on one of those benches,' Kurt said. 'We can speak here with no fear of being heard or being mopped to death by bleach.'

Max sat beside him and waited for whatever questions were bound to be coming his way. The time for clear speaking had obviously arrived.

Kurt sighed. 'I'm sorry. I should have realised that I was putting you all in harm's way. After all, I was the real target, you know. It was me he was trying to kill. I should have known better than to put you kids at risk.'

'Well, I've been thinking about that a lot,' Max said. 'I reckon it was me he was after.' Kurt looked puzzled but let Max continue. 'I saw his face just as he struck the kerb. He was looking right at me and shouting. He's got it in for me, I'm sure. You see, I'd seen him before. It should be me lying in that hospital bed being fed by tubes. Or if Nero had his way, I'd be in a coffin.' Max could have kicked himself. He'd meant to keep quiet and let Kurt do the talking but now he'd let slip that he knew the man's name. Kurt was quick to respond.

'You know more about this stuff than I'd thought,' he said seriously. 'There's more to you than meets the eye. That's why we've got to talk. It's no good us both having secrets when we're both at risk. Divided we fall. United...who knows? I guess it's time we both lay our cards out on the table and have a frank discussion. I can't bear the thought of someone else getting hurt. What do you think, Max? Do you feel you want to talk to me? I quite understand if you don't and I wouldn't want you to feel under pressure. It's just that...'

'If you're happy to tell me the whole truth about why you're here,' Max said, surprising himself with his own bluntness, 'I'll tell you what I can. I must admit I feel very confused. You haven't turned out to be like I expected at all.'

Kurt put his hand on Max's shoulder. 'You're a good kid. I like you. I'm not going to lie to you. Seeing how you looked after Jay while we waited for the ambulance. Seeing how you and Miya get on so well. I'm really impressed with you and I owe you the truth. And after what's happened, I feel you have a right to know more.'

'What about those ice creams in the cinema?' Max was keen to get a few answers straight away. 'I've been dying to ask you about all that stuff. You really did think they'd been messed about with, didn't you?' He waited for the answer, which took a while to come.

'I didn't want you to know about that. I don't want to scare people unnecessarily. But you're right. Yeah, I'm sure someone had just injected something dangerous through the wrappers. Mine definitely had a tiny hole in the seal. I smelt something nasty when I peeled it off.'

'You mean poison?'

'Exactly. Don't ask me how or when he did it. I guess it was in the queue while I fumbled around for loose change.'

'Venom, maybe?' Max waited for a reaction. 'Like a scorpion's?'

'How do you know?' Kurt's eyes flashed into Max's like lasers.

'Know what?'

'Cut the bull. You know full well about the Silver Scorpion, don't you? Who told you?'

Max had expected that question and he'd rehearsed a careful answer.

'A man my dad knows works for the government and they're worried that the Silver Scorpion is planning some sort of attack in this country.'

Kurt didn't look satisfied. 'But how did you know about me and the Silver Scorpion?'

Max knew he would have to lie and he couldn't look Kurt in the face. Instead he turned to watch small children playing 'catch' round the flowerbeds and running barefoot across the grass with innocent squeals and giggles.

'I put two and two together. Dad's friend called round and said a man called Nero from the Silver Scorpion was following him in a white car. I saw him outside our house. I saw him again parked outside where you live, then in the cinema. So I assumed he must be following you, too.' Max was impressed at how calmly he was lying and felt brave enough to ask the big question. He turned back to look Kurt straight in the eyes.

'Are you a member of the Silver Scorpion, Kurt?'

Kurt paused. 'The six-million-dollar question! But it's not a straightforward answer.' Even now he was looking around, staring uneasily at passers-by or glancing suspiciously over his shoulder. 'You can never be sure who might be listening. Let's walk somewhere else. It's best to keep moving.'

They walked through the park.

'The thing is,' Kurt continued, 'I've gotten myself in a mess. When I was a student back in the States I was a hot-head. If there was a protest march or rally I was there. The police had me marked as a political activist. In other words they thought I was trouble. I was very anti-government. That was years ago. I've calmed down since then. Yasmin, Miya's mother, was good for me and we settled down and got on with our lives. But then one of my old radical friends showed up. He wanted me to use my influence to get secret information for an organisation he belonged to.'

'The Silver Scorpion?' Max asked.

'Correct. Not that I knew then who they were. They wanted Yasmin to pass on secrets from where she worked. She had an important job at the Pentagon library where she had access to all kinds of top secret material about defence and the President. Of course we refused to help but things got nasty. Threats and blackmail. So in the end…'

'You ended up spying for the Silver Scorpion?'

'Foolishly, yes…kind of. A few documents, that's all. Just to keep them off our backs. Then, of course, we were in their power. If we didn't help them again, they'd tell the FBI we'd stolen secrets. So it seemed easier to pretend we were friends of the Silver Scorpion. But when we realised they were behind some of the violent terrorist attacks in Europe, we wanted out. That's when things got really nasty and they decided to dispose of us.

Yasmin was the victim. She went to work one morning and didn't come back.' He struggled to speak, taking deep breaths before he continued. 'She fell under a train at the station. I was totally devastated. I know she was pushed but there were no witnesses so her death was declared 'accidental'. I protested and made one almighty fuss but I couldn't prove anything. The police didn't want to hear from a guy with a reputation for trouble. It was a terrible time. It still is. I miss her more than you can possibly imagine.'

'That's terrible. Poor Miya, too.'

'Listen, Max. Miya doesn't know all this. She still thinks her mother's death was an accident. I don't want her scared so don't tell her unless... unless something happens to me as well. I brought her to England thinking we'd be safer here but it seems Nero is after me here now. That's why we've all got to be so careful. And I already know they're planning a terrorist attack over here soon but I don't know what yet. When I do I'll be able to inform your government here.'

'Can't you warn the police or something?' Max was concerned at how scared Kurt looked.

'If only. Nobody wants to listen to the bad guy. I'm an undesirable and "high risk" according to Interpol. I guess I've just got to prove first that I'm not such a bad guy after all.'

'I don't think you're a bad guy. I think you're great!' Max meant it, too and he couldn't wait to send the message back to Tango that Kurt wasn't a member of Silver Scorpion after all. Then everything would be cleared up, he thought. Kurt would be off the black list and Operation Code-Cracker would be over.

'The thing is,' Kurt continued in the softest of whispers, 'this Nero guy isn't the brains behind the Silver Scorpion. No one knows who the boss is.

73

He's a master of disguise and works undercover in the UK. Maybe a double-agent. All I know, he calls himself Telson.'

'Isn't that what a scorpion's tail is called?' Max was quite proud of himself for knowing.

'Exactly. The tip of the stinger containing the venom. The deadliest part of the whole body.'

They sat saying nothing for a while, both lost in their thoughts about the evil Telson.

'Give me a couple of minutes,' Kurt said. 'I'm just going into that candy store to buy a few gifts for you guys.'

As soon as he was on his own, Max sent a text to Tango.

Kurt is not a member of the Secret Scorpion after all. He is not a threat and I have discovered a lot about him. He is in danger from them.

Max wasn't prepared for the reply that came within minutes.

Due to the serious error in your assessment we are closing this phone link. Your services are no longer required. You are dismissed. Get away from him immediately and have no more contact. Operation Code-Cracker is hereby terminated.

Absolutely furious, Max stuffed the phone back in his pocket. 'I've got the sack! So that's the thanks I get.' His phone bleeped and another text came through. It wasn't from a number he knew. All it said was:

HOROBOD BAL

It looked like one of Miya's puzzles but it wasn't from her phone. That was odd. Maybe she'd used her auntie's mobile to send it. Max stared at the letters to see if he could decipher it. This was a tough one and he kept studying it as he and Kurt walked back to the hospital.

They were pleased to see Jay sitting up in bed smiling at the TV, with his mum beside him. 'Isn't Miya with you?' Max asked.

'We thought she was with you. We haven't seen her for ages.'

That was strange, Max thought. He went to the door and peered down the long corridor. The woman who'd been mopping the waiting room earlier was now disinfecting a table. He walked back to speak to her.

'Excuse me,' he asked, 'have you seen the girl I was talking to earlier?'

'No, love. Sorry.'

A voice called out from behind a newspaper. It was the man who'd been snuffling and staring at them earlier. 'Yeah, she left with a bloke. He came in here in squeaky old tennis shoes that left dirty marks over her wet floor. He took the girl off in a white Volvo. It skidded off at a right speed, too.'

Chapter 7
ENTURY

Miya closed her eyes under the glare of fluorescent strip lights in a stark whitewashed underground room. She lay sprawled on the floor, having been thrown onto the green carpet tiles. It looked like some sort of office but there were no windows.

Nero bent over her to rip the tape from her mouth. She whimpered at the pain, as he shouted angrily. 'I'm not untying your wrists. I can see you've already tried to use my mobile. It's no good trying to contact anyone, you fool. It will be too late.'

He looked at the message she'd sent. 'What is this rubbish? You can't even string a sentence together. They told me you were a bright kid but this is gobbledegook. You're not so clever after all. Mind you, if I thought you'd told someone where we are, I'd shoot you right now. Instead I'm going to get information from you, before getting rid of you once and for all.'

He took an empty syringe from a drawer. 'The first injection will be a drug to make you talk. You'll tell me everything. The second will kill you. I'll use the same on your father. I'm about to phone him to tell him where to get his daughter back. Except you'll be dead by then. You're just the sprat to catch the mackerel. It's a trap. The Silver Scorpion doesn't tolerate his sort.' He left the room to fill the syringe.

**

As soon as he realised Miya had been kidnapped, Kurt phoned the police. 'You've got to get here fast and find her. She's in danger. Hurry!'

He paced up and down frantically, unable to speak, while Max tried to make sense of that text message. It must have come from Miya. It looked just the sort of puzzle she would send.

Within two minutes police cars screamed to a halt outside the hospital where Kurt stood waiting. Officers were soon asking questions and looking around the kidnap scene.

'It's no use looking for her here,' Kurt screamed. 'She's gone. Get out there and find her!'

It didn't take long for a woman officer to tell Kurt forcefully that he wasn't helping matters and he would assist to find his daughter far better by explaining everything calmly and clearly at the police station. He was told he would be driven there while officers got on with enquiries at the kidnap scene by questioning all witnesses to the crime. Max watched Kurt being led to the police car and decided it was now up to him to act alone.

He ran out through the main doors and darted into the street beyond the car park. His head was racing with crazy ideas about where he should go. He looked over his shoulder and saw a bus coming so he sprinted ahead to a bus stop and jumped on. He bought a ticket to the other end of town, with no real idea of where to go. It was only as the bus pulled uphill past the library that he realised this was the way to Gran's. She was now his only hope.

***

Gran was busy in the kitchen when Max threw himself through her back door.

'Good grief, Max! Where did you come from?

You're always startling me. Is something the matter?'

Max could hardly speak from being so breathless. 'It's Miya. She's been kidnapped. The police are questioning Kurt. She's in danger. It's the Silver Scorpion…'

'Look dear, calm down. I haven't got a clue what you're prattling on about. Have a drink. I'm just making your birthday cake for Saturday.'

'Gran, not now. This is urgent!' Max was almost screaming. 'I know he told me not to but I'm going to phone Child-Catcher at home. He's got to do something.' He grabbed the telephone directory and fanned through the pages frantically.

'What was his real name? I can't remember, apart from Delta. No, hold on, I think Dad called him Mr Nettles. As in stinging and "ouch".'

He searched through the 'N's before slamming down the directory in sheer frustration. 'Not there. Typical, he's ex-directory. Gran, can you drive me somewhere?'

'Where, dear?'

'I don't know. I'm sure Miya was trying to tell me in this text. Look. You're good at crosswords. What does HOROBOD BAL mean to you?'

'I don't speak Welsh, love.'

'I'm not sure about the BAL but I reckon the first bit is something to do with ROBIN HOOD. You see, there's a ROB inside the word HOOD. That's Rob in Hood. But where can that be?'

'Sherwood Forest? I can't drive that far in my old Morris Minor. I've got no idea what you're jabbering on about.'

'Gran, that horrible man snatched her.'

'Child-Catcher? Is he really a child catcher?'

'No, Potato-head. The one who nearly killed Jay. The one in the Volvo. The one who followed you that time…'

Her mood changed instantly. 'Oh, him. That nasty piece of work in grubby old tennis shoes. A stalker. I'll never go to Archers again.'

Max froze before he screamed, 'Archers!'

Gran put her hands to her ears. 'Max, I really think you ought to – '

'Listen, Gran. Robin Hood was an archer, right?'

'So legend has it but I expect – '

'What's at the back of Archers? The garden centre on the ring road. BAL is LAB backwards. Isn't there some sort of laboratory behind Archers?'

'Oh that place. Behind the high fence. It's some sort of research station. Top secret.'

'In that case…' Max grabbed her handbag and

keys from the hall. 'Drive me there fast. I've got to get her out of there. Go for it.'

'Shouldn't we call the police?'

'Not till we've got there and I've found out if its definitely the place. I don't want to make things worse. I could be wrong – but let's go for it, Gran.'

She shut the front door behind her. 'How exciting, dear. What fun. I've always wanted to do a bit of white-knuckle driving. And I shall tell that nasty Potato-head stalker just what I think when I see him.'

Max had hardly jumped into the front seat of the pink Morris Minor convertible before it squealed from the drive, roared along the crescent and off towards the ring road.

'Neither this car nor I are built for speed, but I'm discovering skills I didn't know I had!' Gran slammed down her foot and almost took the next roundabout on two wheels. 'Make sure that tin of pink paint under the seat doesn't fall over. It's for my new shed. I do like pink.'

A lorry driver waved his fist, while car horns blasted all around them. The traffic lights ahead were on red and Gran screeched to a smoky halt.

'Come on, come on!' Max jumped up and down in his seat. As soon as the lights changed, the car leapt forward with a throaty jet of fumes. Gran pressed a button to open the roof.

'Look!' Max stood up to point ahead. 'You need to turn up that track.' The wind stung his eyes as the car clunked over a speed ramp, knocking him back in his seat. They sped along a grassy track, the spinning wheels throwing up clods of mud as the car chugged behind the garden centre towards trees where a sign in bold red letters was wired to a high fence:

RESEARCH STATION
PRIVATE
KEEP OUT

'Round the back!' Max shouted. 'BAL is back to front. We must use the back as the front.'

Through the fence, almost hidden by bushes, they saw the Volvo parked beside the door of a single-storey windowless building. Gran switched off the engine and they listened. Silence. A security camera pointed at the heavy gates ahead, topped with razor wire.

'Gran, you turn the car round and be ready for a quick getaway. I'm going in there.'

Max leapt from the car and pulled a branch out

of the bushes. He took Gran's car rug from the back seat, draped it on the end of the branch and crept towards the camera, making sure he kept out of sight of its lens. With a heave, he flipped the rug over the camera and smothered it. He reached for his pick-gun and tackled the padlock in front of the blinded camera. Soon the huge gate squeaked open and he sneaked through into the compound. He slid past the Volvo and listened at the closed door. Muffled voices came from inside but he could hear nothing more.

Perhaps there was another way to hear what was going on inside. It was a risk but he decided to try his phone. Maybe Miya could still use the phone she'd used before? He called the number on her last message.

No one answered. Eventually the ringing stopped. When Max heard a click and a buzz, he assumed it was just an answer message about to start. Instead, he heard a grunt followed by a crackle, then a clatter as if the person on the other end had dropped the phone. An image appeared on his screen. The picture was fuzzy at first but he could see tied hands and a close-up of green carpet tiles. It became clear that Miya was lying on the floor and trying to show a selfie. Behind her,

Max could just make out the blurry outline of a man appearing in a doorway.

Their voices came through loud and clear.

'What are you doing?' Miya asked.

'Be quiet. I shall be asking the questions after your injection. Then comes the poison, after which one of my staff will dispose of you. All very simple.'

Max had seen and heard enough. He picked the lock in seconds, gently opened the door and entered a workshop where a man in goggles was working at a bench full of plants: rows of small rose bushes under glass domes. A TV monitor above his head

was dark, with only a faint tartan pattern flickering across the screen. Gran's blanket was doing its job perfectly. Max crawled past him, hidden by a row of cupboards, and then darted down metal stairs into the basement.

A long corridor led to what looked like a kitchen at the far end. There were doors on both sides, all closed except for the end one. Max crept to it and went inside. It was a store room, with bottles of chemicals, powders and shelves of laboratory equipment. He heard a voice through the wall – Miya's voice, which was also coming through his phone. Now he was sure she was inside the room next door.

'I don't know,' she said. 'My dad didn't tell me everything that he found out. He just knew about you, that's all.'

'And did he tell you the Silver Scorpion will become the most feared power of the twenty-first century? Telson will be so proud of me for getting rid of you interfering idiots. As for that kid Max Hunter, I hate the little brat. We're going to finish him off after I've got rid of you. You'll be the first to be eradicated. This injection will see to that...'

There was no time to lose, but Max had no idea what to do – he couldn't just barge in. With that syringe in Nero's hands and presumably a gun as well, the man was ruthless and deadly. The only thing Max had left was the small device hanging round his neck: the distress flare. It wasn't meant for indoor use but he had nothing else.

He rushed into the corridor and to the door of the room where Miya was being held. He dropped to his knees, and punched the air triumphantly when he saw the wide gap under the door.

Snatching off his memory stick, Max pulled out the pin and gently pushed the flare under the door. It was the longest ten seconds of his life as he waited for it to go off. With his face to the floor he could just see Nero's feet as the flare fizzed, spat and erupted in a ball of white light and belching red smoke.

Max saw Nero's feet stamping on the flare. Sparks singed the bottom of his trousers, which he began slapping frantically in a mad attempt to extinguish them. Realising Nero had bent down, Max pushed the door open with the full force of his weight. It slammed into Nero's head with a crack, and he fell back. Blood trickled from his eyebrow as he held his nose, spluttering and choking. Max dashed into the room and frantically pulled the rope from Miya's feet. She stood up unsteadily, holding on to Max with her tied hands as they scrambled for the door. Nero was still on all fours, his nose gushing, but he staggered to his feet, grabbing the syringe and swearing.

Max ran into the corridor, pulling Miya along with him. They darted towards the steps at the end of the corridor, with Nero shouting behind them. A shot rang out with a deafening crack and the metal stairs clanged and sparked in front of them. As they clambered to the top, a man in a lab coat barred their way.

'Oh no you don't,' he growled, waving a metal pipe.

'Oh yes we do,' Max shouted back, grabbing a test tube of liquid from a bench.

'Don't touch that acid, you fool!'

Max threw it down, swishing a spray that fizzed across the floor at the man's feet, sizzling his shoes. He staggered backwards as they barged past him and out into daylight. They could hear Nero clanging up the stairs in his tennis shoes not far behind them, shouting obscenities.

As they reached the gates, more gunshots rang out. The fence crackled around them as bullets peppered the wires, pinging off the metal bars right beside them. Other people had emerged from the building, all with guns. Gran was revving the engine of her Morris Minor. Max glanced back as they reached her and saw Nero at the wheel of his Volvo, gun in one hand and syringe in the other.

Miya threw herself in the front seat next to Gran, who immediately stamped on the accelerator. Through a blast of blue exhaust, Max clambered over the boot of the already accelerating pink car and dived onto the back seat. Dust flew as they shot forwards with a rasping roar.

'Get us out of here, Gran – he's gaining on us!'

'I knew I should have got my dodgy exhaust fixed,' she shouted above the noise, while glancing at her wing mirror. 'Just look at the smoke coming out the back. Max, I hope you don't think I've done a terrible thing...but while I was waiting I was a bit naughty. I let his tyres down. I'm also a dab hand at loosening wheel nuts.'

The Volvo clattered through the gates with wobbling flat tyres and spun round on the track in a dust cloud. The wheels screamed until drowned by ear-splitting metallic clanking.

'He's still gaining on us, Gran!'

A bullet ripped through the back seat and smashed into the passenger's door, just centimetres from Miya's left shoulder. 'Quick, Gran – he's getting too close.'

'That tin of pink gloss paint under the seat, Max. Feel free to chuck it at him.'

Max grabbed it and knelt up on the back seat to see the swerving Volvo heading straight at them. He saw Nero's right hand stretch from the driver's window, taking aim with his gun. Max hurled the tin and watched it slam onto the Volvo's bonnet, splatting the entire windscreen in thick pink paint. Unable to see out, Nero poked his head through his window and accelerated at Gran's rear bumper just a metre in front. He raised his right hand once more, aiming the gun at Gran's head. Without thinking twice, Max wrenched the pin from the second flare round his neck, ripped it off and flung it at the Volvo about to slam into them.

The flare struck Nero's neck and wedged in his collar before erupting in a blinding blaze. In an instant the Volvo veered off the track at terrifying speed. A rear wheel spun off and flew through the air as the front bumper smashed into a speed ramp. The car flipped upwards and twisted in mid air, crashing down with a roar and shattering of glass. Instantly the airbags inflated and within seconds the car crunched on its side before juddering to a halt, its remaining three wheels still spinning noisily. The flare's spewing sparks and belching red smoke sputtered into feeble puffs drifting on the breeze.

The silence that followed was eerie…before Nero, spattered in pink paint, slumped through the open windscreen and rolled onto the mud. He gripped his gun with both hands, staggered drunkenly to his feet and aimed it directly at Max. But he didn't pull the trigger. Instead he looked down with horror at the syringe sticking out of his leg. With nothing more than a whimper, he lurched across the grass like a zombie. He sank to his knees, dropping the gun, then crumpled face down in the mud. His arm twitched and he lay still in the lingering silence.

The long stillness was suddenly broken by a final sputter from the flare fizzing under the rear tyre, where a trickle of liquid slowly snaked from the ruptured fuel tank. With one last cough of sparks, the flare ignited the petrol dribbling across the grass. An angry roar ripped through the car, which instantly erupted in a massive ball of flame. The explosion echoed all around as thick black smoke rolled across the sky.

Miya looked at Max. 'Wow! That was close. By the way, you could have got here sooner – what kept you?' She grinned cheekily.

'Your weird text clue!'

'Then what do you make of this one?' She took Max's mobile and texted ENTURY.

'And what is that supposed to mean?' But before she could tell him, he shouted his answer. They ended up chorusing: 'Long time, no see!'

Gran turned to giggle at them, swerving the car across the track and slamming her foot down on the accelerator once more, and they roared towards town, coughing thick acrid smoke behind them. Right then their carbon footprint was the last thing on their minds.

Chapter 8
10 ISSUES

By the weekend, Max's birthday party threatened to be an anticlimax after all the recent excitement. Police, newspaper reporters and TV crews at last drifted away to find other heroes to annoy. Kurt and Miya, having slept off their exhaustion, relief and endless writing of police statements, could at last get on with more pressing affairs, like helping Max's dad with the birthday barbecue. Gran, as always, kept a close eye on the finer details by making sure each guest brought a brand new football. The lawn was soon littered with them, under a haze of wafting charcoal smoke.

Mum, just back from her travels, arrived with an exotic tan and an enormous trifle. Miya caused cheers by giving Max a *Spy Kids* DVD and a set of puzzle books, just before Jay arrived on his crutches, with a bright purple leg plaster and a beaming smile. The hugs and applause went on for some time until Max tapped a spoon on the picnic table and made a point of clearing his throat exaggeratedly. 'Ladies and gentlemen, allow me to say a few words of thanks. Unaccustomed as I am to public speaking…'

Everyone cheered and banged their cutlery.

'Please – I would just ask you to keep the noise down. After all, we wouldn't want to disturb the neighbour…' At that point a football flew over the fence from next door and landed with a thud in a flower bed. More cheers. Gran chuckled and blurted in an unsubtle stage-whisper, 'I told you Child Catcher wasn't what he seemed. There's more to him than we thought.'

Max laughed, 'I think I may have to go round there and complain…' But before he could continue his rehearsed speech, the doorbell rang.

'Don't worry, I'll answer it.' Dad left the barbecue, followed by Max after he'd given a quick bow to enthusiastic applause. He scurried into the kitchen to peer through to the front door, where a smartly dressed man in a pin-striped suit stood on the doorstep.

'Good afternoon.' He spoke in a crisp, no-

nonsense tone. Max caught a glimpse of a shiny black Mercedes parked at the kerb behind him, with a chauffeur sitting in the driving seat.

'I think it's next door you want,' his dad said.

The stranger smiled. 'It's this address I've come to visit, Mr Hunter. I would like to speak to Max. I've come from Downing Street where the Prime Minister asked me to call.'

'Right. Blimey. You'd better come in. Max! Er…we're just having a bit of a party.'

'I promise I won't keep Max long, Mr Hunter.'

Max was summoned to the sitting room as Delta from next door arrived. The two men spoke in hushed whispers at the door before joining Max, who was waiting patiently on the sofa. The stranger in the suit stepped forward to shake his hand. 'I'm from MI6 and have just come from Downing Street where your recent escapades have been brought to the attention of the Prime Minister. I've come to pass on the Government's thanks and congratulations for a job well done, Max.'

Before Max could say anything, Delta spoke – but with a more tetchy edge.

'I'm afraid I have to apologise about a certain misunderstanding on our part. It seems our department failed to accept your assessment of Kurt. In short, they didn't believe you the other day. A slight error, I'm afraid.'

'You told me British Intelligence didn't make mistakes,' Max grinned. 'I've never been given the sack before. If you weren't ex-directory I'd have phoned you to sort it out.'

Delta's eyebrow twitched slightly, betraying his annoyance. 'No one ever gets my spelling correct. I'm the only Netols in the book. N-E-T-O-L-S. I'm of Huguenot ancestry.'

Max was close to joking about Huguenots and 'huge nose' when the MI6 man butted in. 'Both Mr Netols and I regret the communication problem, but you coped admirably. If only more youngsters were like you, Max. You have a clear sense of right and wrong, which I find most impressive. You have also enabled us to make many arrests. The Silver Scorpion will never be the same again. Nero told us everything – surprisingly, he wasn't too badly hurt after his crash. Injecting himself with his own truth drug seemed to loosen his tongue beautifully. He responded most favourably to our questioning procedures. I believe the expression is 'hoist by his own petard'. He will now serve a considerable custodial sentence.'

'Prison!' Max grinned. 'Brilliant. Nero behind bars at last. Potato-head has had his chips!'

Delta sat in an armchair, carefully aligning the toes of his highly-polished shoes. 'I'm afraid I can't join your garden party, Max. Business to attend to. Thank you for inviting me and I wish you many happy returns. You'd better get back to your guests. Don't be too noisy and annoy the neighbour, eh?'

'I'll try not to. Otherwise he might nick my football again or send spies round in the middle of the night.'

Delta smiled awkwardly, seeming rather distracted as he left the room.

The MI6 man glanced out of the window towards the waiting Mercedes. 'Look, Max, if ever you'd consider doing more work for us, I'd be most interested to hear from you. Here's my card. Youngsters like you are hard to come by. Thanks to you, we should be closer to uncovering the brains behind Silver Scorpion, the one known as Telson. You've helped upset his plans but he's bound to strike again. You could be the one to flush him out from wherever his headquarters might be. We'll let you know if there's any way you can help us again – if ever there's a case to crack that's just up your street.'

Once more the man shook Max by the hand, before leaving. After watching the Mercedes glide away, Max turned to give Gran an exuberant high-five. 'I've got a job as a spy-catcher!' Then, in a slightly shaky New York accent, he croaked, 'The name's Hunter. Max Hunter. I'm the new Telson-buster.'

Gran could only smile, being more concerned with arranging the garnish on a rice salad.

Max returned to the smoking burgers on the patio before running across the lawn and kicking one of the footballs to Dad. 'Come on, Dad, see if you can score for Villa!'

Dad headed it back and Max leapt spectacularly to deflect it from slamming into the top corner of the goal. The ball flew up, bounced on the top of the fence and dropped over the other side. 'Oops!' Groans from the spectators.

When everyone resumed their conversations, Max slipped quietly indoors, through the kitchen to the front door, as Gran called after him.

'Where are you going, dear?'

'Just popping next door to see if I can get my ball back.'

She laughed. 'Don't start all that again!'

Leaning against Gran's shiny pink car on the front drive, Max looked up at the rambling house next door. His gaze wandered from one window to another. It didn't seem quite so scary now that he knew the sinister goings-on inside were only in his dream. Maybe Child-Catcher was human after all, for there, still poking up by the front door, was that little wooden cross with the letters R.I.P. carved lovingly across it. By the single word LOVE engraved in its marble base lay the solitary white rose. Despite his coldness, the man living there must have a warm heart for someone he'd lost.

Max stood for a long time just staring, imagining how things could have turned out very differently.

The light began to fade and a cool breeze stirred the rhododendrons. Miya appeared on the doorstep and waved before sidling up to him. 'You're looking thoughtful,' she murmured.

'It must be terrible to lose someone special,' he said. 'Poor old Mr Netols.'

Her eyes followed his gaze to the cross on its engraved marble plinth.

'Weird place for a grave. For a loyal pet, I guess.' Her mood brightened as she squeezed his hand. 'Hey, mister birthday boy. One last puzzle.' She showed him the letters: IO ISSUES on her phone screen.

Max smiled. 'Would it have something to do with Potato-head, by any chance?'

'Possibly,' she chuckled.

'Then I reckon it could be his grubby footwear. Ten Issues or "tennis shoes".'

'Correct again! Who's a clever boy, then?'

Max tapped the keypad. 'See if you agree with this one.'

1 2 3 4 5

ME

Before she had time to work it out, Max beamed. 'You can always count on me, honey.'

Miya giggled. 'You bet, my hero.'

She rested her head on his shoulder, slid her arm round his waist and cheerily led him back indoors.

EPILOGUE
TONELESS TONSIL

The danger was far from over.

Icy fear returned with the darkness in Max's bedroom at midnight. Fragments of recent conversations suddenly fused together in his latest dream. Whispers drifted through his brain and familiar voices gabbled louder and louder. A cry echoed through his nightmare and he woke with a start.

The Child-Catcher had returned.

Heavy with sleep, Max struggled to sit up. He held his breath, trying to hear above the thumping in his chest and the rushing of blood in his ears. Was the sound of Bach out there in the night or just in his head? His throat tightened, as he remembered the words spoken just a few hours before by the man from MI6. 'We'll let you know if there's any way you can help us again – if ever there's a case to crack that's just up your street.'

Max suddenly realised the awful truth and, as he sat shaking in the solid darkness, he was aware that he was the only one who knew...until his phone bleeped beside him. He snatched it and squinted at the text from Miya.

OMG – just worked it out. Can't talk – phone prob bugged. Mega teethed theme won.

His brain was still reeling. It was a struggle to concentrate on Miya's weird anagram. After minutes of scribbling on a notepad, he turned MEGA TEETHED THEME WON into MEET ME AT THE HEDGE NOW.

He knew which hedge she meant – the high one outside Jay's house, with the hiding place inside. He got dressed, grabbed his torch, crept downstairs and slipped out into the night. After wheeling his bike silently from the shed, he cycled off to his meeting, along deserted roads in the misty darkness. As he pedalled frantically, the words from his dream echoed through his head again and again to the rhythm of his breathing. Both voices at once: Gran and Mr Netols.

'I told you he wasn't what he seemed. There's more to him than we thought.'

'Codes and anagrams are my business. I'm the only Netols in the book. N-E-T-O-L-S.'

A dingbat flashed like a beacon in his brain: BCDFHIJKLMOPQRSUVWXYZ x 2

***

Miya was waiting by the hedge. 'Quick, inside.' They scuttled into its dark interior where prying eyes, microphones and the orange glow from the streetlamp could not reach.

'I was a fool not to get it quicker,' she whispered. 'It's the white rose that did it. Then I worked out the anagram of R.I.P. CROSS IN LOVE. That grave thing by Delta's front door.'

'I think I know what you're going to say,' Max interrupted. 'It's only just clicked with me, too.'

'At the lab they were cultivating unusual silvery white roses. They handled them with such thick protective gloves, I wondered if the thorns had some sort of poison. The point is, I'd never seen roses quite like them before – apart from on that grave thing by Delta's front door. Do you realise R.I.P. CROSS IN LOVE is an anagram of SILVER

SCORPION? The house next to your dad's is their headquarters. Delta is a double agent. He's the boss. He's Telson – an anagram of Netols.'

Her chilling whisper was followed by a more chilling silence. They couldn't see each other's faces, but they still sensed each other's mounting fear. Child-Catcher had been the evil mastermind all the time. He'd been with them only hours before. They held hands tightly, sitting in the darkness, thinking of the frightening truth that only they knew.

Max murmured almost inaudibly, 'Miya, you're a genius. Mind you, I must be, too – as some of that clicked with me! That's why I brought the MI6 man's card with me. I think I should phone him right now. I'm so glad I've got you with me.'

Miya squeezed his hand. 'Yesterday you were 10 but now you're 11. No more zero – no more Nero – you're my hero! Come on, we'll do this together.'

For the second time she rested her head on his shoulder, slid her arm round his waist and slowly led him indoors.

Did you crack the anagram for the last chapter?
TONELESS TONSIL = ?

NETOLS IS STOLEN
Or
TELSON IS NETOLS
(But don't tell anyone – it's top secret!)

Airlock
Simon Cheshire

George, Josh and Amira are visiting a space
station when a massive explosion destroys almost
all of the station, and most of the crew. Trapped in
the wreckage, hurtling towards Earth, can George
and his friends figure out who's to blame?
And will they make it back alive?

ISBN 9781408196878   £4.99

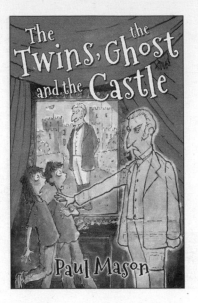

The Twins, the Ghost and the Castle
Paul Mason

When runaways Tom and Stella secretly move
in to a real castle, they think all their problems are
over. But they're dead wrong. For a start, the castle
is haunted. And although the ghost turns out to be
a lot of fun, their happy home is soon threatened
by a destructive developer and a mean-spirited
ghost hunter. Can the twins help the
ghost – and save their castle?

ISBN 9781408176269   £4.99

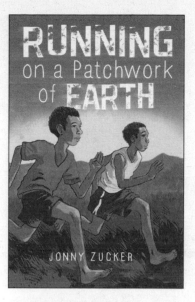

RUNNING on a
Patchwork of **EARTH**
Jonny Zucker

AK is one of the star runners in his school.
A shining athletics career beckons until his father's
job suddenly drags the whole family from Kenya
to cold, rainy London. Now AK has no friends,
no coach, nowhere to run, and a whole lot of new
problems to handle. But there's help on offer, and
maybe even friendship. Can AK patch together a
new life in England – and start to win again?

ISBN 9781472905345   £4.99